To Cleere – RS

For Monica – GW

Buster's Echo
Text copyright © 1993 by Ragnhild Scamell
Illustrations copyright © 1993 by Genevieve Webster
First published in Great Britain by ABC, All Books for Children,
a division of The All Children's Company Ltd. under the title *Woof! Woof!*
Printed in Hong Kong. All rights reserved.
1 2 3 4 5 6 7 8 9 10
❖
First American Edition, 1993

Library of Congress Cataloging-in-Publication Data
Scamell, Ragnhild.
  Buster's echo / by Ragnhild Scamell ; illustrated by Genevieve Webster.
    p.   cm.
  "Willa Perlman books."
  Summary: A dog, a rooster, a cow, and a mouse mistake their own echoes
for larger animals and set out to scare them away.
  ISBN 0-06-022883-0. — ISBN 0-06-022884-9 (lib. bdg.)
  [1. Animals—Fiction.   2. Echo—Fiction.   3. Animal Sounds—Fiction.]
I. Webster, Genevieve, ill.   II. Title.
PZ7.S2792Bu   1993   92-29868
[E]—dc20   CIP
                                                      AC

Buster's Echo

• By
Ragnhild Scamell

• Illustrated by
Genevieve Webster

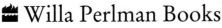 Willa Perlman Books
An Imprint of HarperCollinsPublishers

Each morning, Buster
went into his garden and
barked, "Woof! Woof! Woof!"
   And across the valley, a large
dog answered,
"WOOF! WOOF! WOOF!"
   One day Buster decided to go chase him away.
And he trotted down the hill.

Soon he met a rooster. "Have you ever seen
the large dog that lives across the valley?" Buster asked.

"That's not a large dog," said Rooster.
"That's a giant rooster. Cock-a-doodle-doo!" he crowed.

"COCK-A-DOODLE-DOO!"**
replied the giant rooster from across the valley.

"There must be a large dog *and* a giant
rooster across the valley," said Buster.

"I'll go with you to chase them away," said Rooster.
And off they went.

Soon they met a cow.
"Have you seen the large dog and the giant
rooster that live across the valley?" Buster asked.

"No, but I have heard a
terrible bull. Moo!" Cow lowed.
"MOO!"
roared the terrible bull from
across the valley.
And Cow followed Buster
and Rooster down the hill.

"Where are you
going?" said a little mouse,
who just managed to skip out of their way.
"We're going to chase away the large dog, the
giant rooster, and the terrible bull that live across
the valley," said Buster.
"That's not a large dog, or a giant rooster, or a
terrible bull," laughed Little Mouse. "That's a mean rat."

"Squeak!" he peeped, and
pricked up his ears. "Listen!"
No one else could hear the mean rat,
but they were too polite to say so.

"There must be a large dog, a giant rooster, a terrible bull, *and* a mean rat across the valley," said Buster.

"I'll go with you to chase them away," said Little Mouse.

And off they went—Buster, Rooster, Cow,
and Little Mouse—across the valley and all
the way to the top of the next hill.

But where were the large dog, the giant rooster, the terrible bull, and the mean rat?

"Woof!" barked Buster.

"WOOF!" answered the large dog from the other side of the valley just outside Buster's house.

"Cock-a-doodle-doo!" Rooster crowed.

"COCK-A-DOODLE-DOO!" replied the giant rooster from just outside Rooster's yard.

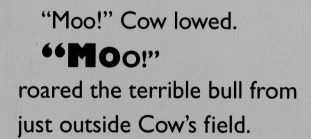

"Moo!" Cow lowed.
"Moo!"
roared the terrible bull from
just outside Cow's field.

"Squeak!" peeped Little Mouse.
And still no one could hear the
mean rat's reply, but they were too
polite to say so.

"They've sneaked across to *our* hill because they are so scared!" said Buster. "We must go back home and chase them away."

So off they went back home across the valley.

"Woof! Woof! Woof!" barked Buster,
as he struggled up their own hill.
But the large dog answered,
"WOOF! WOOF! WOOF!"
from the other side of the valley!

"We've chased them away," said Buster proudly.

"Cock-a-doodle-doo!" Rooster crowed as he puffed up his feathers.

"**COCK-A-DOODLE**-DOO!" replied the giant rooster from across the valley.

"Moo!" Cow lowed.

"**MOO!**" roared the terrible bull from across the valley.

"I don't think there was a mean rat after all," Little Mouse peeped.

Rooster went back to his hens.

Cow went back to her field.

Little Mouse disappeared down a hole in the ground.

And Buster trotted
back to his bed.
"Good-bye!" he shouted.
"GOOD-BYE!**"**
answered the large dog from
across the valley.